Mr. Lippincott, Mr

Old Wonder-Eyes and Other Stories For Children

outlook

Mr. Lippincott, Mrs. L. K.

Old Wonder-Eyes and Other Stories For Children

1st Edition | ISBN: 978-3-75234-386-1

Place of Publication: Frankfurt am Main, Germany

Year of Publication: 2020

Outlook Verlag GmbH, Germany.

Reproduction of the original.

OLD WONDER-EYES;

AND

OTHER STORIES FOR CHILDREN.

BY

MR. AND MRS. L. K. LIPPINCOTT.

Old Wonder-Eyes.

Once, when I was in England, I visited some friends, who lived in a pleasant part of the country. They had a fine old house, filled with all sorts of beautiful things; but nothing in-doors was so delightful as the wide, green lawn, with its smooth, soft turf, and the garden, with its laburnums, and lilies, and violets, and hosts on hosts of roses. There was a pretty silvery fountain playing among the flowers, so close to a little bower of honey-suckles that the butterflies fluttering about them had to be very careful, or the first they knew, they got their wings soaked through and through with spray.

About the house and grounds were all kinds of beautiful pets—greyhounds, and spaniels, and lap-dogs, and rare white kittens; gay parrots, and silver pheasants, and sweet-singing canaries; but here, in this pleasantest spot, right under the honeysuckle-bower, all alone by himself, in a large green cage, sat an ugly gray owl. He was the crossest, surliest old fellow I ever saw in all my life. I tried very hard to make friends with him—but it was of no use; he never treated me with decent civility; and one day, when I was offering him a bit of cake, he caught my finger and bit it till it bled; and I said to Mrs. M——,

"What *do* you keep that cross old creature for?"

I noticed that my friend looked sad, when she answered me and said—

"We only keep him for our dear little Minnie's sake—he was her pet."

Now I had never heard of her little Minnie—so I asked about her, and was told this story:—

Minnie was a sweet, gentle little girl, who loved everybody, and every creature that God had made—and everybody and every creature she met loved her. Rough people were gentle to her, and cross people were kindly; she could go straight up to vicious horses, and fierce dogs, and spiteful cats, and they would become quiet and mild directly. I don't think that anything could resist her loving ways, unless it were a mad bull or a setting-hen.

One night, as Minnie lay awake in her bed, in the nursery, listening to a summer rain, she heard a strange fluttering and scratching in the chimney, and she called to her nurse, and said,

"Biddy! what is that funny noise up there?"

Biddy listened a moment, and said,

"Sure it's nothing but a stray rook. Now he's quite gone away—so go to sleep wid ye, my darling!"

Minnie tried to go to sleep, like a good girl; but after awhile she heard that sound again, and presently something came fluttering and scratching right down into the grate, and out into the room! Minnie called again to Biddy; but Biddy was tired and sleepy, and *wouldn't* wake up. It was so dark that Minnie could see nothing, and she felt a little strange; but she was no coward, and as the bird seemed very quiet, she went to sleep again after awhile, and dreamed that great flocks of rooks were flying over her, slowly, slowly, and making the darkness with their jet black wings.

She woke very early in the morning, and the first thing she saw was a great gray owl, perched on the bed-post at her feet, staring at her with his big, round eyes. He did not fly off when she started up in bed, but only ruffled up his feathers, and said—

"Who!"

Minnie had never seen an owl before; but she was not afraid, and she answered merrily,

"You'd better say 'Who!' Why who are you, yourself, you queer old Wonder-Eyes?"

Then she woke Biddy, who was dreadfully frightened, and called up the butler, who caught the owl, and put him in a cage.

This strange bird was always rather ill-natured and gruff, to everybody but Minnie—he seemed to take kindly to her, from the first. So he was called "Minnie's pet," and nobody disputed her right to him. He would take food from her little hand and never peck her; he would perch on her shoulder and let her take him on an airing round the garden; and sometimes he would sit and watch her studying her lessons, and look as wise and solemn as a learned professor, till he would fall to winking and blinking, and go off into a sound sleep.

Minnie grew really fond of this pet, grave and unsocial as he was; but she always called him by the funny name she had given him first—"*Old Wonder-Eyes!*"

In the winter time little Minnie was taken ill, and she grew worse and worse, till her friends all knew that she was going to leave them very soon. Darling little Minnie was not sorry to die. As she had loved everybody and every creature that God had made, she could not help loving God, and she was not afraid to go to Him when He called her.

The day before she died, she gave all her pets to her brothers and sisters, but she said to her mother—"*You* take good care of poor old Wonder-Eyes—for he'll have nobody to love him when I am gone."

The owl missed Minnie very much; whenever he heard any one coming, he would cry "Who!" and when he found it wasn't his friend, he would ruffle up his feathers, and look as though he felt himself insulted. He grew crosser and crosser every day, till there would have been no bearing with him, if it had not been for the memory of Minnie.

The next time I saw the old owl, sitting glaring and growling on his perch, I understood why he was so unhappy and sullen. My heart ached for him—but so did the finger he had bitten; and I did not venture very near to tell him how sorry I was for him. When I think of him now, I don't blame him, but pity him for his crossness; and I always say to myself—"*Poor old Wonder-Eyes!*"

Old Horace,

AND

MY LITTLE PIG HUMPY.

A deep, broad, lazy-flowing river! It is one of the loveliest things in nature. When I was a little boy I lived near one, and among my very pleasantest memories are those of the days when I fished, and swam, and dived in its clear deeps, or sailed my tiny boats and played "dick, duck, drake" over its sleepy surface.

About half-way up the hill-slope which made the western bank of this river, stood our house. It was a large, dark old building—somewhat gloomy-looking on the outside, may-be, to a stranger; but *inside*, even in the most out-of-the-way corners of those great rooms, there was no gloom—the sunshine of peace and love made light everywhere. The dear old home!

Among my father's servants there was an old negro, who, as occasion required, was, by turns, coachman, gardener, carpenter, and house-servant. His name was Horace; he had no other name, I believe—at least, I never knew of any. Horace was one of the blackest negroes I ever saw, and as large-hearted as he was black. He was very fond of children, and very good-natured usually, though not always, as you will see, by-and-by.

Horace could make the nicest little wagons and sleds, and the clearest, sweetest-toned willow whistles in the world, I used to think. He could tell to a day, almost, and without trying them, when the May-duke cherries had reached their luscious prime; he could remember, from year to year, exactly in which row, and how far from the end, the early-ripe apple tree stood; he knew too, the very moment, I thought, when the frost had opened the chestnut burrs and ripened the persimmons, so that they would not pucker up our mouths, as they did sometimes, when we were so foolish as to think we knew better than he; he could pick out the luckiest places for our rabbit-traps, and could always find worms for bait, no matter how dry the weather, when we wanted to go a-fishing. In short, Horace knew everything, it seemed to me then.

At the time of which I write, I was eight years old, the younger of two brothers, and Horace's favorite. He used to say that my rosy, chubby face, black, saucy eyes, and laughing, rollicking, topsy-turvy ways, were "better comp'ny" for him than the more thoughtful, quiet, sober bearing of my brother Walter.

Walter went to school in the village, which was about a mile from our house, over the hill; but I said my little lessons to my mother, at home, an hour every morning and afternoon.

When it was not lesson-time, Horace and I were nearly always together; no matter what he might be at work on, he could usually contrive to find something to please me and keep me near him.

One morning, while I was saying my lesson, my father had given Horace a severe scolding for his forgetfulness, which was the only fault he had, I believe, but it was a most grievous one, and often led to serious trouble. After I had finished my lesson, without knowing anything about the scolding he had had, I went out into the garden, where Horace was working, and asked him to fasten a wheel on my little wagon, and help me to gear up my dog, Branch, to it.

"No! go 'long—I'se busy!" said he, without looking at me, and puffing out his great lips. Then he added, in a muttering way, to himself, "Nebber did see sich a bother as dese yer boys is!"

I was rather a passionate boy, and this roused me at once. I said something saucy back to him; then he said something else; then I said something in return, ending by calling him "an old nigger," and went back to the house.

Nothing could have offended Horace more than that "old nigger," which had slipped off my tongue in the heat of my passion, and for which I was heartily sorry a moment after—for, like a great many other negroes I have known, although he frequently called himself so, he would suffer no one else to.

All day long he did not speak to me, nor look at me, though I made a pretence of having several errands to the garden and went right by him—and at night I went to bed quite unhappy about it.

The next morning, I moped about the house, and tried to amuse myself with my humming-top, but it would not spin to suit me, and I threw it aside pettishly and went down to the kitchen, to ask old Wangie, the cook, to tell me a story, while she washed the breakfast things.

I found Wangie and Horace, with the other servants, still at their breakfast; so, without saying anything, I went up to the window and began to blow my breath against the glass, and make figures on it with my fingers. Once I turned my head, and found Horace looking at me with an earnest, wistful look that seemed to say, "I am ready to make up;" but I was proud, and could not bring myself to say anything—though a little soundless voice down in my heart kept urging me to, and though I knew I had been most in fault—until just as Horace was getting up from the table, when the little voice overcame my pride, and, tilting one of the loose flag-stones of the floor up and down with my foot, I said, without looking at him,

6

"Horace, I ain't mad at you, if you ain't mad at me." When I had got thus far I felt so much better that I looked up frankly into his face, and added, "And I am sorry I called you what I did."

"Lor' bress de chile!" said he; "Ise sorry too. I know'd de boy couldn't stay mad at ole Horace long, and ole Horace couldn't at him, sartin. But ye see, Mass' L——, when you com'd to me I was busy; and den Mass' B—— had jis been talking sharp to de ole nigger, 'cause he forgit to take de gray pony to be shod. I tells ye what, Mass' L——, it make ole Horace feel 'siderably bunkshus[A] for a leetle bit; but Missus says we must forgib and forgit. De Lor' knows I kin do de *forgittin'* part so well, 'tain't no use to say nothin' 'bout t'other. De ole nigger all right now, though, and he got de purtiest sight to show de boy he ebber see in all he born days."

[A] This is one of Horace's own words, and I never heard any translation of it.

With that he picked up his hat, took me by the hand, and off we started, the best of friends again.

How well I remember that day! It was in the middle of May, and the sunshine was so warm and bright, the sky so clear and blue, and the grass, as we passed through the orchard, looked so beautiful, with here and there a snowy drift of apple-blossoms, into whose honeyed hearts the little pilfering bees were diving—and the birds sang so joyously, and such fragrant prophecies of the golden summer-time came floating to us upon every breath of the wind, that I said to Horace, I thought it must be a Sunday that had slipped out of Heaven, by mistake.

"Dun'no, Mass' L——," said he; "but I 'spec dey don't make no mistakes up dar."

During this we were crossing the orchard toward a little closely-fenced lot, about an eighth of a mile from the house, in which were the sheep and pig-pens.

I was not yet perfectly well assured of Horace's good humor, and so, although I was terribly curious to know, I had not dared to ask him where we were going, or what we were going to see.

Horace carried a pail of milk, which he had picked up as we passed the milk-house, in one hand, while I had hold of the other with both of mine, and was jumping and swinging along, when, just after we had entered the enclosure and were passing one of the large pig-pens, he set down the pail, and taking me at one of my jumps, with a slight lift of his brawny arm, set me up on the edge of the pen, exclaiming—

"Look dar now, boy! Wasn't ole Horace right—aint dey de purtiest little tings y'ebber did see?"

Right down under me lay the old sow, and rollicking and rooting, and butting and squealing around her were eight of the prettiest, darlingest, cutest little pigs that ever saw the sunshine.

One little fellow, black all over, was lying by himself, with his head lifted up a little, so that he could see me. This one did not seem so glad and spry, and fat and saucy as the others, and there was something in his look that brought a warm feeling to my heart, and made me pity him.

"Well, Mass' L——, which one's ye gwine for to choose for your'n?" said Horace, after I had sat there some minutes.

I looked at them all, except the little black one, again, and finally decided upon a pert, head-over-heels sort of a fellow, that was racing up and down the pen as furiously as though he had had a coal of fire fast to his tail, and was trying to run away from it. Every once in a while he would stop short, as if he had forgotten something, and suddenly remembered it—then he would look up at me in the most quizzical way imaginable, with his little impudent eyes, give a snort, a quick jerk of the head, and away again. He was as white as snow all over, except his tail and one ear, which were black. He seemed to understand that I was going to make a choice, and to be determined that I should choose him; and this frolicking and frisking were his ways of "showing his paces," I suppose; or else his funny little black tail was twisted up so tightly that he couldn't keep still.

Just as I was turning around to say to Horace that I chose that one, something, I did not know what, made me look down at the little black ugly one again. He was still looking up at me, with a sick, sad, hopeless, yet patient look, and at once it seemed to me that I heard that little voice again—heard it with the ears of my heart, as it were—"Choose him!"

I turned around to Horace, who seemed to be getting impatient at my taking so long to choose, and said very quietly, and somewhat sadly, perhaps, for I remember that my voice and the way I spoke seemed to astonish him as much as my choice—"I'd like to have that one for mine, Horace."

"What! Mass' L——! y'ain't gwine for to take dat ar little pigininny! Why he ain't o' no 'count, no how!—an' he look sick too—mebby he die. Let ole Horry choose for ye. I'd take de little feller wid de black tail and ear,"—pointing to the one I had fixed upon at first—"he's as peert as a jack-knife; and den, white's a mighty sight purtier color dan black—dat is, for *pigs*," added he, catching himself, for one of Horace's hobbies was the notion that black was "de best color in de world for folks."

But all Horace said about the little pig looking sick, and that "mebby he die," only made the little voice beg the more earnestly—"Take him! take him!" and

I said to it, softly—"I will," and to Horace, aloud—

"Please let me take the little black one, Horace. I want to nurse him and make him well, like the others."

Horace looked a little displeased at what he thought was wilfulness in me, but said nothing more. He then took up the pail and poured the milk into the trough—my father being of the opinion that it was never too early to begin to feed pigs. At once the little fellows—all save mine, who lay still and alone, only turning his strangely sad eyes from me to the trough—made a furious rush towards it, crowding, squealing, and pushing like—so many little pigs as they were, and like nothing else in the world. Some plunged their heads into the milk, clear up to their eyes, which fairly twinkled and snapped with roguery, and one—the one with the black tail and ear, scrambled into the trough bodily, just as though he wanted to get more than the others, and thought he could absorb it with his legs and body, as well as take it in at his mouth; then, not satisfied with this, he went marching up and down the trough, treading on the snouts of his fellows, until they got angry, and rooted him out entirely.

I wanted to take mine up to the house and give him some warm milk and nurse him, but I saw that Horace was not much pleased with him, and I was afraid of renewing our quarrel by proposing it then.

More than a week passed, with my going down twice every day with Horace, to feed the funny, noisy little rascals, and staying there more than an hour sometimes, to watch them eat, and frolic about the pen. After the first day, I made so bold as to ask Horace to let me take some warm milk in a little old pan, for mine. He consented, and would even get over into the pen and hand him out to me, while I put him down on the ground, in the sunshine, and scratched his back and head while he ate, until he grew to know me, and Horace grew to like him and to be as anxious about him and as tender toward him as I was.

As I said, more than a week passed in this way, when, one morning, Horace said he should let them take a little run outside. So he propped up the sliding door with a stick, and drove the old sow out, while the little pigs came tumbling after. I stayed a long time, watching them root and frisk about—mine always lagging behind the others and never playing any—till it came dinner-time, and I went up to the house. After dinner I went with Tom (one of our hired hands), over to the mill, and did not get back till tea time. Just as I was getting into my place at table, I heard a squeal from the kitchen, and with the thought of my pig in my mind, rushed down to see what was the matter.

Horace had just come in and was standing by the fire, with Wangie and Tom, looking at my poor little pig, who lay on an old bag in his arms, dead—as I thought, till Horace, in laying him down on a chair, jarred him a little, and made him squeal again.

He had fallen down into an old dry cistern there was in the sheep-yard, and broken "he right *hand* foreleg," as Horace said.

"Betta kill um," said Tom—"he not werry fat, but'll do to roast for de kitchen."—Tom and I had never been very good friends, and you may be sure that this speech did not help to make us so.

"Go 'way, boy!" said Horace, whose heart was always as gentle as a girl's; "he Mass' L—— 's pig, and he gwine for to be doctored."

Horace's idea struck me, and without thinking, without my hat—the tears streaming down my face, and nearly dark as it was, I took piggy in my arms and started off toward the village, to find my uncle, who was a physician.

Just as I got to the gate at the end of the lane, I met him riding over to take tea with us.

"What's the matter—what have you got there, and where are you going at this time of the day?" asked he, somewhat startled by my singular appearance.

"Oh, uncle!" said I, "I'm *so* glad you've come.—Why it's my little pig, and he fell down the cistern and broke his leg, and I was just coming for you to mend it."

"You had better let me open his carotid," said he.

"Will that make him well?" asked I.

"Yes," said he, "it'll take all his pain away, and he won't know his leg's broken two minutes after I do it."

"Oh, I'm so glad you can do that!" said I.

At this, my uncle laughed heartily, for he had been making fun of me all the time—the carotid being one of the most important arteries of the body. It supplies the brain with blood, and if he had opened it, poor piggy would have bled to death in a minute; that's what my uncle meant by saying it would take away all his pain.

In spite of his joking, my uncle was a very kind-hearted man, and after he had finished laughing at my simplicity and ignorance, he got off his horse and put the bridle over his arm, saying—"Your pig's too heavy for you; besides, you should carry him with his legs up,—it will lessen the flow of blood to the wounded one, and so save him a good deal of pain,—let me take him."

He seized hold of the little fellow, who had lain perfectly quiet since I had taken him, except now and then a low, piteous moaning, which always started my tears afresh; but the instant my uncle touched him, he began to squeal terribly, and struggle, till uncle said that if I could carry him, may be I had better, for the struggling would irritate the broken leg. So he let go of him, and he was quiet again in a moment, except that plaintive moaning which seemed almost like human sobbing.

About half-way up the lane, we met Horace, whom my mother had sent out to see what had become of me. My uncle told him to get some little thin pieces of hickory, and showed him how to make some splints. He then told him to take little piggy, thinking I would not be strong enough to prevent his struggling; but he squealed and took on so in Horace's hands that I insisted on holding him, and to the surprise of all, he only squealed once during the whole operation. There seemed to be a magnetism in my affection which soothed and lessened his suffering; just as you may remember when you were sick, if your dear mother or aunt laid her hand on your forehead, or stroked your hair back, or smoothed your pillow, it seemed to quiet your pain, and drive it away almost entirely for the time. I think little pigs can feel this as well as little folks, and my little pet understood that I loved and would let no harm or hurt come to him that I could prevent; and that is why he did not squeal when I held him.

Several weeks passed by before my uncle thought it safe to take the splints from piggy's leg; during which I fed and tended him constantly. During this time also, the doctor discovered that the fall had injured his spine too, which he said would prevent his growing much, and would cause his shoulders to gradually hump up.

Sure enough, it was not long before we noticed that a regular hump had begun to form, just behind his shoulders, which led to his being called Humpy. My father first called him so in sport, and though at first I was very indignant, because it seemed like making light of the poor little fellow's misfortunes; yet the name got fastened on to him, in spite of Horace and me, and finally we fell in with the rest, and called him Humpy too.

In the mean time, by his patience and gentleness through all his long, tedious illness, by his quick appreciation of kindness and bright intelligence, he had made himself the favorite of the whole household—even of my father, who usually declared pigs to be "disgusting." Still I continued to be his special and particular friend; next to me came Horace, and we two gave him his baths in warm soap-suds, two or three times a week, which always pleased him amazingly, and kept him as clean as a baby. He would follow me like a dog, through the garden, all over the house, up and down stairs, pat, pat, pat, and if I did not notice him frequently, he would set up a funny little squeal, and crowd right against my heels. I frequently woke from my afternoon naps that summer, and found him snuggled down by my side. I taught him to stand up on his hind legs, and beg for pears and apples, and to lie down and pretend to be dead, and several other funny tricks. I frequently took him with me when I went to ride. He never could be prevailed upon to lie down, at such times, but would insist upon standing on the floor of the vehicle, where he would pitch and stagger about in a way very funny to see.

All the dogs, and cats and everything and everybody about our establishment, seemed to have a kindly feeling toward Humpy, with the exception of a little bantam hen of mine. She for some reason, possibly because she was rearing her first brood of chickens, took a dislike to him and flew at him every time he came in her neighborhood. One day as Horace and Wangie were sitting at dinner and I was blowing soap-bubbles out of the window, we heard a terrible squealing in the hen-yard, and on rushing out to see what was the matter, found the little bantam perched on Humpy's back, pecking away at his ears, like the little shrew that she was, and he, the little simpleton, was standing stock still, and squealing for dear life. Horace speedily rescued him from his perilous situation, but it was a long time before he could be coaxed into the hen-yard again.

Almost the funniest thing about little Humpy was his manner of sleeping. The day after his leg was broken, Horace had made a snug little low box for him, and filled it with wool for his bed, and though Wangie was very particular about her kitchen, she had become so attached to the little fellow during his sickness, that she suffered the box to remain, and as it drew near winter, she would even place it by the fire of nights. About eight o'clock in the evening, and often earlier, Humpy would scramble into this box, and instead of lying down on his belly or side, as little pigs all the world over do, he would turn over on his back, with his little legs sticking up, and so sleep all the night through. This always amused our visitors greatly; it seemed as though they never would be done laughing at it, and indeed it was extremely funny.

Fire, from first to last, seemed to be a profound and most fascinating mystery to Humpy. Frequently, in the early evening, he would station himself just in front of the great open kitchen fire-place, and stand by the half hour looking straight into the roaring flame. I used to say at such times, that he looked like the picture of Napoleon by his camp-fire, the night before Austerlitz, though nobody else could see the resemblance.

Snow was another thing which he never seemed to quite understand. Our first snow-storm that winter came in the night-time, and in the morning, when Wangie opened the door for him to take his airing, he seemed to be really frightened at first, and she had great difficulty to get him out. But he soon grew to like it, and finally nothing would please him better than to put him out where he could run and frisk and root in it, and he would look so cunning when he came in afterwards, with his eyelashes all filled, and his little black head and snout all stuck over with white patches. The sound of sleigh-bells, too, was evidently a great delight to him, and the sleigh never drove up to the door that he did not rouse up and frolic about till the door was opened, when he would rush out upon the piazza. Sometimes we would take him in the sleigh with us, when he would take his stand in the bottom with his snout resting on the side, and so ride for miles.

But, poor Humpy! his little troubled day of life was almost done.

"Hog-killing time" had come, and great kettles of water were kept constantly over the kitchen fire, to be heated for scalding the animals after they were killed. As Horace and Tom were lifting one of these off, it slipped and tilted over, pouring more than a gallon of the boiling contents right into Humpy's bed, which, owing to the busy tumult of the day, I suppose, had not been moved away.

The poor little fellow was just taking his morning nap.—I will spare you and myself pain, by telling the rest as briefly as possible.

In a few minutes the whole household had collected in the kitchen. Horace had wrapped the little fellow in a blanket, but I saw my father shake his head as he looked at him, and taking Horace aside, whisper something to him, to which the tender-hearted old man answered aloud,—

"No, Mass' B—— don't ax ole Horace to do dat ar, 'cause he couldn't, no how."

Father then called Tom and whispered to him, and afterwards to my mother, who took me softly by the hand and asked me to come with her to the sitting-room, where she explained to me that Humpy was too badly hurt this time to get well, and told me what father had whispered to Tom.

She had hardly finished, when I heard the crack of the pistol in the direction of the barn,—it almost seemed to me that the ball had gone through *my* heart.

Horace laid my little dead pet in the old box of wool, nailed it up, and we buried him with all the household by, at the foot of the garden, under a sickle pear tree, the fruit of which *he* had liked best.

And what became of dear old Horace?

After Walter and I went away from home, a great change came over Horace; he grew silent and reserved, and liked to be alone a great deal, and finally, with his savings, he bought a small tract of land, on the top of one of the highest hills in the neighborhood, where he built himself a little house and kept a great many goats. One morning one of his nearest neighbors, on going out, found some ten or fifteen goats at his door, bleating most piteously. Knowing that nobody thereabouts kept goats but Horace, and suspecting that something was wrong, he called one of his men and started over to Horace's house. When they got there, they found Horace lying on his bed, his hands folded peacefully across his breast—dead.

The Rooster-Mother.

A LITTLE STORY FOR THE LITTLE ONES.

Once on a time there lived in a country farm-yard, a plump, pretty, gay-feathered hen, who among all the fowls was the liveliest scratcher and the merriest cackler, except when she was setting on a nest full of eggs, when she was so cross that there was no coming near her—always squalling and bristling up on the slightest provocation. She had a particular spite against the young pullets who had no such domestic duties to confine them, but could go gadding and cackling about just as they pleased.

She always appeared to be in a terrible hurry to have her brood hatched and started in the world; and those poor weakly or lazy chicks who were the last to get out of their shells, she was apt to treat very unkindly.

One time she sat on ten good eggs, and in one day hatched nine fine chickens. But the shell of the tenth egg remained unbroken for some time longer. At last, after a good deal of pecking and rolling and kicking about, it popped open, and a puny little cockerel crawled out—"peep," "peep"-ing in a scared pitiful way, that ought to have touched any hen-mother's heart. But this proud biddy seeing that he was so small and ugly, and being very angry because he had kept her waiting so long—coolly turned her back on him, and devoted herself to her stronger and prettier children. That night, she refused to brood him, and actually drove him from the nest. If it had been cold weather I think he would have died,—but though such a wee, young thing, he had sense enough to see that if his mother would do nothing for him, he must look out for himself,—and as he could not nestle under her wing, he determined to make the best of her tail-feathers. So under their shelter, he managed to keep tolerably comfortable till morning. After that the hen treated him a little better —but she often scolded him and clawed him, and he led a sad life. Many times, when the children flung crumbs to her and her brood, she would drive this poor little half-starved chick away, and he would run and hide in the currant bushes, and hang his head, and droop his small tail, and may-be wish that he had never been hatched.

Now, it happened that there was also in that farm-yard a good old rooster, who, observing how cruelly the little cockerel was treated, resolved to adopt him. So one day, he took him under his protection; he hunted grain and worms for him, fought for him at meal times, and *even brooded him at night*, till the unfortunate chick was old enough to roost.

Under his care the puny young cockerel grew strong and handsome, and my little readers will be glad to hear that he always treated his good old rooster-mother with kindness and respect. As for his own mother, you will be glad also to hear that he once had the opportunity of defending her from a fierce rat. He went at it, with beak and spur, and soon drove it bleeding and squealing into its hole.

Then the hen was happy to make up with him; and his brothers and sisters were very fond and proud of him ever after.

My Aunt's Present.

When I was a little girl I was very backward in all my studies. I should not like to be obliged to tell how old I was before I was able to read without stopping to spell out the long words.

We had then living near us an aunt, my father's only sister, a kind, good woman, whom God took home to himself only a few months ago. Well, this aunt felt great concern about my backwardness, as her own children, who were all grown men and women then, had been remarkably forward and clever, and her grandchildren were wonderfully learned little creatures. Once, while on a visit to us, when I was about eight years of age, she called me up to her, and put me through a short reading lesson.

I can remember, even now, how shocked she looked when she found that I could not read so well, nor half so fast as her five-year-old-grandson—a conceited little gentleman, who seemed very well pleased to surpass me. As for my aunt, she regarded me curiously through her round-eyed spectacles, as though I had been some wild girl of the woods. I looked down, and began twisting and biting my apron-string, while I tried to excuse myself by laying the blame on my unfortunate lisp, and my poor eye-sight. But my sensible, straight-forward aunt replied that the fault all lay in my idle, romping habits, and my love of pets and play.

I was deeply mortified, as I had a great respect for my aunt W——, for I knew that she was good and clever, though sometimes a little too dignified and stern, I then thought. I grew very red in the face, very hot in the throat, and finally burst into tears. This touched my aunt's kind heart at once, and drawing me toward her, and parting the thick, dark hair from my forehead, she spoke gentle, encouraging words to me, all in her own short, quick way though, which startled, almost as much as it soothed me. She said that if I would apply myself diligently to my books, play less and study more, so as to be able to read to her on her next visit, a chapter in the Testament, without making a single blunder, she would bring me a nice, new story-book, from the city of New York, where she was about to spend a few weeks. I laughed through my tears with joy and gratitude. I gladly promised all she asked, and thanked her heartily; for in those days, and in the country village where we lived, a new story-book, or indeed a new book of any kind, was a very rare treat. If I could only hope that this little volume would be thought half as much of, as I used to think of my books, I should be very proud and happy to-night.

My aunt seemed pleased with my pleasure; her handsome eyes did not look severe or reprovingly any longer, but smiled softly through her spectacles. She patted my head quite tenderly, and inquired kindly after the health of my pet dog, Fido. I brought him to see her, and I wanted much to bring also my pretty kitten, Katurah, for this was in her day—but my aunt, with all her kind-heartedness and piety, had one peculiarity which always grieved me—she never could abide cats.

My dear uncle was different in this important respect. He was very friendly with kittens, or perhaps made believe so, because of my great liking for them, and not wishing to hurt my feelings, in this or any other matter. He was the most beautiful, as well as the most lovable old man I have ever seen. He was tall, erect, broad-chested, with silver-white hair, smiling mouth, and pleasant brown eyes. He was never known to speak, or look harshly at any one; and though he was a minister, and a very learned man, I never was afraid of him in the least.

I remember that one winter, I spent a whole fortnight at the parsonage. It was the longest time I had ever been away from home, and when I went back, I was a little mortified that they did not make a great ado over me, and that my brothers and sisters did not notice how much I had grown.

During this visit, my good uncle used every evening at twilight, to set me up on his shoulder, and walk slowly up and down the drawing-room. I was light and slender, and sat very securely on his broad shoulder, with one arm around his neck and the other clasping my kitten. It was not a frolic—we were quite still and quiet. My uncle repeated Scripture softly, and studied out his sermons, while I thought about my home, and kitty purred. But we all enjoyed ourselves amazingly. On Sundays, when I sat in the minister's pew, listening to my uncle's solemn preaching, I felt a sort of pride in the sermon, as though I had helped to make it,—which was very foolish certainly, as after all, kitty had done quite as much as I toward it.

The parsonage was about five miles from our house, and my uncle and aunt used to drive over to see us in an old-fashioned, two-wheeled chaise, which they had brought with them all the way from Connecticut.

This vehicle, which I suppose was nothing extraordinary, seemed to me then something almost awfully grand. It was varnished very bright, and there was a good deal of brass about it, so whenever I saw it coming up the street, flashing in the sunlight, it appeared to me like a splendid golden chariot, fit for a king. Indeed, when, last summer, I saw the gorgeous state-carriage of the Queen of England, I hardly thought it as magnificent as that same old chaise of my uncle's had once seemed to my childish eyes.

It was a great treat for me to be taken by my uncle and aunt, for a little drive down the street, in this chaise, which rocked back and forth so softly that I always wondered how they kept awake in it till they got home. Perhaps they did not, but left everything to their steady old white pacer,—and safely enough, for "sober Sam," as we called him, always seemed to know that he was a minister's horse, and behaved accordingly. On the day of the visit, when my aunt had made the agreement with me in regard to the book, they let me go with them further than usual, allowed me to hold the reins, and even to touch up with the whip, the fat and lazy old pacer. So unused was he to such treatment, that, I remember, he stopped short, and looked round to see what was the matter.

I returned home through the bright sunset time, singing and skipping—took my Testament at once and read until after eight o'clock; only stopping to feed my kitten and put my dolls to bed.

From that time I daily and diligently studied my reading lessons in the New Testament. I preferred the stories of the miracles, and Christ's beautiful Sermon on the Mount, for practice—as the affecting part of the Gospels made me cry so hard that I could not read correctly.

Many and many were the bright hours during that summer, when I stayed in from play, that I might earn that new book. I denied myself frolics with Fido, I neglected the domestic affairs of my play-house, and let my dolls get shabby, all for the sake of my promised present.

At length, I found myself able to read whole chapters without making a single mistake—and my mother encouraged me to believe that I should certainly win the prize.

Finally, we heard that my aunt had returned from her visit to the east, and early one afternoon, we had the happiness to see the old white horse and chaise bringing my uncle and aunt up the road.

I, with the others, was very much delighted to welcome our visitors, but on my own account, rather nervous and excited to think that my trial was so near. Two or three times that afternoon, I stole out of the room to glance over my Bible lesson. I hardly know whether I most dreaded or longed to be called upon for my reading, and to have it over.

Soon after tea, my aunt sat down in a window seat, and called me to her side. Without many words, I took my little Testament from my pocket, opened at the fifth chapter of Matthew, and began reading very glibly,—"*And seeing the multitudes, he went up into a mountain, and*"—

"Stop!" said my aunt, "you must not choose your own place to read—it's my business to do that!"

She then took the book from me, and actually opened at the first chapter. Now, my dear children, you remember, don't you, what this first chapter of Matthew's Gospel is? It is made up almost entirely of the hardest kind of Scripture names—many of which I should not like to be called upon to read aloud, even now. I felt my heart sink at once, and already mourned my book as lost. But I went to work quite calmly—I conquered four or five of the first names, then I began to stammer—then paused to spell them out in my mind— then stopped altogether.

My aunt said "a-hem!" and looked at me over her spectacles, with a queer, quizzical, "I've caught you!" sort of a look.

I dropped my head in shame and perplexity. My aunt sat still and stern, and awfully silent. At length, I looked up through the long hair that had fallen forward over my face, and said, as coaxingly as I knew how—

"You know, dear aunt, these are the names of great kings and patriarchs—and it's not just proper to read them over fast—is it?"

"Ah, you naughty girl," she replied—"that is a foolish get-off—it won't do. You cannot always expect to choose where and what you are to read. A *good* reader will be at home anywhere. It is plain you do not deserve the book."

I was wretchedly disappointed and mortified; but I did not cry this time. I was too indignant for that. I did not plead for the lost book. I said nothing at all, but went out calmly enough to the gate, with the rest, to see our visitors off.

This evening my aunt did not invite me to ride in the chaise, but took my little brother Albert instead. I was sorry for this—not that I would have gone, but I should have liked to have drawn myself up to my full height, and to have said —"No, I thank you, Mrs. W——." She kissed me, as usual, but I did not kiss her back—and I thought she felt it. I fear that I did not kiss my uncle very affectionately, though I knew he was not to blame.

I lounged about the gate for awhile, and made believe I felt very much at my ease—then I went out into the garden and sat down behind some lilac trees, and buried my face in my apron, and went off into a good hearty cry. I also relieved my hot, angry heart, by talking to myself, something in this petulant, passionate way:—"Oh dear, it's too, too bad! such fun as I have given up to get ready for this reading—so much good time wasted! It wasn't fair—it was right down mean in her to set me at those long, hard, crooked names, that never ought to be read—that never ought to have been made at all! She's mighty proud of knowing so much Scripture—just as if a minister's wife could help it! I don't love her—I'm glad she's gone—*I* don't want to ride in her old chaise!"

In the midst of this fit of passion and ill-humor, my pretty white kitten came to me and rubbed against me coaxingly, purring very softly. But I let her purr away, and took no notice of her. Fido came bounding along, and, crouching down beside me, began rooting under my arm to get at my face, and licked my hand and whined, till, I am ashamed to say, I got out of patience, and gave him a smart slap on the jaws. He sprang up indignantly, and went and laid himself down under a currant bush, to pout. Then I hid my face in my apron again, and went on with my crying.

All at once, I heard my little brother calling me, from the other end of the garden. But I did not move—I did not answer him —but only muttered to myself—"It's too bad; they won't leave me alone a minute—they are all against me—I can't even *cry* in peace." But soon I heard his voice and his step coming nearer. Then he stood over me, saying joyfully—

"Sister, sister, see here, what auntie sent back to you! She had it in the chaise-box all the while!"

I looked up, and down into my lap was dropped *such* a beautiful book, with a bright red cover, and gilded leaves, and hosts of fine pictures! I was half beside myself with joy. I jumped up so quick that I overturned my brother, and trod on kitty's tail. I hastily begged pardon of both, and then ran off to Fido, to make friends with him. But a slap on the jaws was the one insult that he never would forgive in a hurry. He put on a doubly injured air and sullenly refused to receive my apology; though it was as handsome a one as I knew how to make. I took him by the paw and told him how sorry I was for what I had done—then I patted his head caressingly—but he turned over toward the currant bush, and his tail never wagged an inch. So I left him to pout it out, while I ran into the house to show my gift to mamma and the rest.

They all thought it exceedingly pretty, and said that my aunt was very good to give me so handsome a present, for so poor a performance. I thought so too, and felt troubled in my conscience for not having kissed her, when she went away. I forgave her for the fright she had given me—but, I grieve to say, I had a sort of spite against those good old kings and patriarchs for a long time after.

As soon as I grew sufficiently calm, I sat down and looked through my book. It was a volume of Natural History, Travels, and Wonderful Adventures. Oh! how plainly I remember to this day, every picture it contained. There was one of an old Turk, sitting cross-legged, on a carpet, smoking a great pipe, with such a long winding stem that I wondered the smoke didn't get lost in it. There was a Chinaman, with his hair braided in a long tail that nearly touched the ground—so that if he should step backward suddenly, he might trip himself up. And a Chinawoman, with such tiny little feet that if it had not been for the name of the thing, she might as well have had no feet at all. Then there was a picture of Noah and his family entering the ark—all crowding in as though in a hurry to get out of the rain; and another of a happy Arab family, sitting in their tent, with their horse in the midst, which quite put me out of conceit with houses. Indeed, I proposed to my brothers, to fasten a blanket upon hop-poles and camp out that very night. They all said that it was a brave plan, the only objection being that we had no warm sand to sleep on, and no kind, gentle pony to keep us company—our old gray mare having a young colt, and being always particularly cross at such times. Then there were portraits of wonderful animals and serpents, the like of which I had never seen; there was a boa-constrictor, winding himself round and round a poor antelope, and squeezing him so tight that I almost listened to hear the bones crack. There was a giraffe, stretching his long neck up and out as though to look over the hills to see the sun rise. There was a family of apes on a tree, enjoying themselves, chattering and eating nuts, and swinging by their tails; and a kangaroo mother running away from a tiger, and carrying her little ones in her apron. There was an angry elephant tugging at the body of a great tree, to get at a hunter who had wounded him. I remember how surprised I was on inquiring for his trunk, to find that this was only the common name of the great proboscis which he held before him, for I had been so foolish as to suppose that he carried it on his back, or strapped on behind him.

I treasured up this volume for years and years. I loved it all the better for the grief I had suffered when I supposed I had lost it by my poor reading, and though I have had hosts of handsomer and more costly books since, I have never had one I prized half so highly as My Aunt's Present.

A Curious Dog Story.

A great many anecdotes have been told of dogs, from Ulysses' faithful brute, who, although his master was away twenty years, fighting the Trojans and wandering about the world, did not forget him, but kept one glad wag of affection in his old tail for his return, then dropped dead—down to the "Neptunes" and "Neros," the "Lions" and "Carlos" of which everybody knows;—but we once heard one which we think very few, if any of you, can have heard.

A friend of ours had three dogs,—two tolerably big ones and one little one. The big dogs he had had several years, but the little one, a Scotch terrier, had been bought only a few months before the time I am telling of.

About half a mile from our friend's house there was a mill, and the miller kept a large mastiff dog, who had always been very quiet and peaceable, until just about the time this little terrier came into the neighborhood, when there began a succession of battles between the mastiff and our friend's two big dogs. These battles became so frequent and so fierce, that they attracted the serious attention of both the miller and our friend.

What could it be that had made of these dogs such sudden and bitter enemies? Nobody could tell. But the poor creatures were never without a lame leg, a torn ear, or hurt eye; for as soon as the wounds of one battle got well, and often before, there would be another, even more bloody than the last, until our friend made up his mind that he must either shoot his dogs, or give them away to somebody that lived farther from the mill.

One bright morning, while things were in this condition, the miller was leaning out over the half-door of the second story of the mill, when he noticed our friend's little terrier trotting down the road, with his ears and tail set up very gaily. He thought it queer that the little fellow should be so far away from home alone—so, without exactly knowing that he did so, he watched him. He came running along, first on three legs, then on four—in that funny way that little dogs do, sometimes, you know—right down to where the miller's dog was lying stretched at full length in the sun.

The miller's dog took no notice of him at first, but kept lazily blinking his eyes and now and then snapping a saucy fly off his side; but the little dog began to walk around and around him, apparently saying something, in dog-talk, which seemed to make him uncomfortable, and to gradually rouse him up and make him angry, for he stuck up his tail and bristles, and began to walk around too, growling and looking very ferocious. This seemed to be all the little terrier wanted, for he trotted off up the road, leaving the other to growl to himself. The miller then went to his work, forgetting all about the matter until some ten minutes afterwards, when chancing to look out the door, what should he see but the little terrier, followed by the *two big dogs* of our friend, running toward the mill, and looking as though they were a good deal excited about something.

Thinking it possible that the trouble between his own and neighbor's dogs might now be explained, he went to the door and carefully watched the movements of the animals.

Our friend's two big dogs followed the little one until they came just opposite the mill, when they stopped in the road, bristled up their backs, and began to walk round and round after each other, snarling and looking dreadfully savage, while the little terrier went over to the miller's dog, who had already begun to put on his fierce looks, and entered into a growling conversation with him, which grew more and more violent, till the two parties got nearer and nearer, and finally pounced upon each other, and began a most terrific fight. As soon as this was accomplished, the little terrier coolly seated himself in the sun by the mill, to "see it out."

The secret was out at last. The little terrier had been playing the part of mischief-maker between his master's and the miller's dogs, just for the pleasure of seeing them fight. He had gone down to the miller's dog, and told him, probably, that our friend's two dogs had said that his tail was not so long as theirs, nor, consequently, his coat so fashionable, nor were his manners so elegant; neither, being only a miller's dog, was his position in society so distinguished as theirs—nor was he altogether so well-bred and gentlemanly a dog as either of themselves.

This, of course, would make any miller's dog who was so foolish as to be sensitive about such matters, very angry; but a sober-minded, cool-headed miller's dog, would first, before getting angry, have found out whether all these things were *true*; if so, he would then have ever after treated our friend's two dogs with the silent contempt they deserved. But it seems this miller's dog was not sober-minded, or cool-headed, for he at once got very angry, and turned about, and said a great many insulting things of our friend's two dogs, which the little terrier very carefully remembered, and trotted back and repeated to them, with some nice little additions of his own. Whereupon they too—without thinking whether this little trickstering Iago of a terrier was not imposing upon them, appear to have immediately declared their intention of chastising the insolence of this low-bred miller's dog; which intention we suppose the little terrier ingeniously applauded, so that they allowed him to lead them off by their noses, as it were, to the mill, where they got into a fight, and got sorely bitten by the miller's dog (who was bigger than they, and had a much *longer* tail), besides being thoroughly drenched with cold water by the miller himself, as did also the miller's dog—just as they all deserved, for being so silly and foolish as to take everything that a little gossipping busy-body of a terrier had told them for truth.

Is there not a moral somewhere in all this?

Willie Watson.

Once on a time, I cannot just say when, but it was years on years ago, there lived near a pleasant village in England, a nice, kind-tempered, elderly woman, whom the neighbors called "dear old Dame Watson." She was not rich, this worthy dame, but she would never allow herself to be called poor, for as she had a comfortable home, and was industrious and healthy, she never felt want. She was a very neat seamstress, and so diligent and obliging that she never lacked employment.

Dame Watson was a widow and childless, but she had living with her, two orphan children of her youngest son. William Watson was long the comfort of her sad widowhood, but when he grew to be a man, he chose the hard and dangerous life of a sailor. After awhile there came a long war-time, and there was fighting on the sea as well as on the land, and at last poor William was killed in a battle between two great ships. Then he was let down into the deep sea, to where the water is always still and clear—where the drifting silver sand covered him like a grave-mound—where the long sea-weed waved over him like grass, and bright mosses and beautiful shells shone round him like flowers.

When the news of the brave sailor's death reached his home, his mother, who had seen a great deal of trouble and learned to submit to God's will, bowed her head and prayed; and soon the good Lord gave her strength, so that she wiped away her tears, and went about her daily duties; but William's young wife was ill and weak and could not bear her grief, but pined away fast and died, leaving a little daughter and a baby son to the care of their grandmother.

These children were a great charge to the good woman, you may depend—but still they comforted her, and made the cottage cheerful; so she never fretted about the trouble. Kitty Watson was a bright, intelligent, good-tempered little girl, and so rosy, fat, and funny that nobody could look at her without smiling. Kitty was handy and industrious, and for all her merry, frolicsome ways, was a great help to her grandmamma, in the cottage and garden.

Willie grew to be a fine handsome hearty child, full of play and laughter and chatter, and was the pet and darling of the whole neighborhood.

The cottage garden was very small, yet, with care and industry, Dame Watson was able to raise in it not only vegetables enough for her own use, but a few choice salads, peas, and cauliflowers, which she disposed of to the Rector of the parish, whose learned old gardener could not grow anything so fine, though he boasted that he once gardened for a real lord.

At first, Dame Watson used to carry these to the rectory in a hand-basket, but at last, she hit upon a plan for saving herself time and trouble. She had a house-dog that was the petted playfellow of little Willie, and which she treated kindly for the child's sake, though she had no love for dogs in general, and Bran's laziness and voracious appetite tried her very much. Now, she resolved to make him useful, so she had a little cart and harness made, and taught him to draw the baskets of vegetables from the cottage to the rectory, with Kitty for a driver or leader. Bran was strong, though he was not very large—he was good and intelligent, and always did the best he knew how. The widow said that though the dog grew thin and had pretty much given up frolicking, she knew he must be happier in his conscience for earning his living; but perhaps Bran had his own private opinion on this matter.

One morning, little Master Willie insisted on riding over to the rectory on top of the load of vegetables. There he sat, grand as a lord, flourishing his whip over poor Bran, who pulled and panted along and thought his lot was a very hard one indeed, almost too much for patient dog-nature to bear. And so it was, for the baskets were uncommonly heavy—Willie was fat, and Kitty too full of frolic to think of helping, even by pushing when they were going up hill. But how Willie enjoyed his ride, selfish, thoughtless little fellow! He laughed and shouted and flung his arms about, and bounced up and down, and kicked with delight.

The next morning, when they were getting ready to send the baskets over to the rectory, Bran's harness was found so gnawed and torn that it could not be used. The widow said that the rats had been at it—but Bran, naughty dog, knew better. The good dame had a new one made, but when she went to put it on to Bran he gave a dreadful howl and ran away, as fast as he could. After a day or two, he came back, bringing a huge mastiff, which he introduced to his mistress, as a better cart-horse than himself. The widow was so much amused by this cunning trick that she made use of the stray mastiff and let Bran go back into his old lazy ways.

I cannot stay to tell you any more of Willie's childhood. He was always a good boy at home, and a diligent scholar at school; so everybody liked and respected him. When he grew to be a young man the good Rector got him a situation in a London counting-house. There he always remembered his grandmamma's teachings, and was prudent, industrious, and honest; so he rose and rose, till he became a great, rich merchant, and was knighted by the king. He married a beautiful lady and they had children—some half dozen I believe, and I have heard that they were all handsome and clever and good. Kitty Watson never married, but she always had a pleasant home with her brother.

At last Sir William (for that was his title now) bought the estate on which his grandmamma's cottage stood, and built a fine house on it. He would not have the cottage torn down, but kept it carefully for the dear old dame's sake, though she had been gone to Heaven ten years or more.

The first time that Sir William and his family drove over to the rectory, in their grand yellow-bodied coach, with a big-wigged coachman on the box and two footmen in smart liveries behind, the good merchant said to his sister —"Do you remember, Kitty, my first ride over this road on the little dog-cart? Oh never, never have I enjoyed a ride half as much as that. I never shall have such another, for I never can be *little Willie* again."

The Tale of our Kite.

One bright October afternoon, when I was about twelve years old, for some reason there was no school; so half a dozen of us went out into a great field that adjoined our play-ground, to try a new kite which we had hired one of the big boys, who was a great hand at such things, to make for us.

It was a handsome round-headed kite, with a broad jolly face very cleverly painted on it. Because of this face, we gave it the name of "Diddle Diddle Dumpling," in honor of that old rhyme, in which a youth named "John" is said to have gone to bed with "one stocking off and one stocking on."

The first time we tried to raise it, like the negro minstrel's chicken, its "tail" was "too short to fly high," and it went darting and pitching and bobbing its jolly head about in so many directions, and in such queer, drunken ways, that if we had not known Diddle to be a most proper individual, we should have supposed he had been taking something to drink, and it had "gone to his head." But, as I said above, the trouble was not with his *head*; and besides, although it is the nature of kites usually, to "get high" whenever they have a chance, we knew that Diddle had never got so.

After we had added another bob or two, and pinned (I was half afraid the *pin* would make him dart about more than ever) a tuft of slashed paper to his tail, we tried him once more.

One boy climbed up on the fence, and held Diddle as high as he could—another held his tail, which was already squirming about, but I think it was the wind and *not* the pin, that made it—while I held the string and was to do the running. When they cried "Ready!" I started, at the top of my speed, across the field towards the woods, which were about a quarter of a mile off.

At the first bound I made, up shot Diddle like a rocket, with his long, graceful tail streaming behind him;—up, and up, and up, till the distance seemed to rub his jolly face out. First the laughing wrinkles disappeared, then his eyes, then his fat rosy cheeks melted away; and, last of all, his fiery nose went out, and there was nothing to be seen of our kite but a little speck floating like a bird away up in the blue heaven.

By this time we had almost reached the woods, and had climbed up on a fence to rest, and watch Diddle.

We had not sat there long, before *bang!* went a gun just behind us. We had been so still, and the report was so sudden and so near, that we were nigh tumbling off the fence from the shock. We turned around just in time to see a

31

flock of blackbirds rise out of the woods like a drift of black leaves carried up by a swoop of wind. At first they rose almost straight up into the air, and then swept away over the school-house, directly toward our kite, which they soon hid from our sight entirely.

Some minutes passed before we got sight of poor Diddle again, and very soon after we decided that it was time to get him down and go home. So I began to pull in the string, while the other boys took turns in winding it up.

Nearer and nearer he came; but just as his flaming nose began to show itself clearly, we noticed a black spot which seemed to be almost directly over it. We all wondered what this could be, for we knew it was not there when Diddle went up.

Faster and faster I pulled in the string, and nearer and nearer came the kite, when what should the spot be but a dear little *blackbird*, perched quietly on the upper rim of it! But what made him sit there? we wondered. Why didn't he fly away and join his companions, that were now just vanishing into the far distance? Nearer and nearer it came, to our very feet.—

He was dead!

One little crimson drop that had rolled down his glossy breast, and fallen upon Diddle's cheek, like a tear of blood, told the story. He had been shot.

Poor little bird! He had flown up with the others, and had tried to follow them; but, faint with pain and bleeding, he could not keep up, and so, as the flock was passing our kite, he had settled down upon that, hoping, may be, that the pain in his little breast would get better soon. But, alas! his gold and crimson wings were never again to beat the sunny air as he piped his blithe gossip to his dusky-winged mate: they were folded at his sides, and would be still for ever.

We did not say much to each other, and what we did say, was in a lower and softer tone than usual; for the piteous history of the little bird had touched our hearts.

At first we decided to make a little coffin and bury him. But, suddenly, I remembered that my uncle, the doctor, sometimes stuffed birds and animals; so I proposed that we should go to him, tell the story, and ask him to stuff our blackbird. Uncle was a kind-hearted man, and, after listening to the story, which he said was a very singular one, he promised to stuff the bird.

In about ten days he gave it back to us, looking almost alive. We took it, fixed its little feet on the kite, just as they had been, and persuaded our teacher to put it up on the top of his mineral cabinet; and there it stood all the rest of the time I went to that school.

May be it stands there yet.

Philip Annesley's Return.

It was a stormy November night, many years ago, in an old town in old England. Without, the wind howled and the rain poured, but within the happy and comfortable home of Doctor Annesley, all was quiet, warmth, and brightness. A cheerful circle was gathered round the hearth. There was Doctor Annesley himself, a tall, handsome man, standing in the ruddy firelight, tossing the baby in his arms, while two young children, a boy and a girl, stood before him, one affectionately clasping his knee, yet both, with their father, listening respectfully to their Grandpapa, old Sir Hugh Annesley, who was relating a story of his boyhood. By a table sat Mrs. Annesley, the Doctor's good and beautiful wife, busy with her sewing, yet not too busy to attend to the low-voiced talk of her eldest son, a noble boy of about ten years.

"It seems so strange, mamma," he said, "to think of Grandpapa ever having been a little boy like me! 'tis harder a great deal, than to think of my tall papa as small, like brother Harry, because *he* has such long beautiful hair, and such a full, rosy face, and can laugh and play as merrily as any boy. So could Uncle Philip. But Grandpapa has thin, white hair, and such dim, deep eyes—he stoops and trembles, and looks very sad sometimes. He scarcely ever plays with us, and never laughs in the merry way he used to, when Uncle Philip told him funny stories. I wish Uncle Philip would come home! Why don't he, mamma?"

"Hush, Herbert!" said Mrs. Annesley in a low tone, "remember, I have told you to be very careful not to speak of *him* before your Grandpapa. Your Uncle Philip was a wild, passionate, self-willed boy, and though we all loved him dearly, he has caused us much sorrow by his misconduct. He was Grandpapa's youngest, darling son, yet gave him a great deal of trouble by refusing to do as he wished to have him; and finally, almost broke his heart, by running away from college, and going to sea. Several years have passed since we heard from him, and it is sorrow and anxiety about him, more than old age, that has whitened dear Grandpapa's hair, dimmed his eyes, and bowed him toward the grave. This, my love, is the reason that you must not speak of your Uncle Philip."

Just at this moment there came a quick ring at the door, and a servant soon entered, bringing a message to the Doctor. A sailor, just off the sea, was thought to be dying of fever at the hospital, and had sent for him.

Dr. Annesley did not hesitate for an instant to leave the comfort and pleasant talk he was enjoying, to go where duty called him through the tempestuous night, and not one of his loving family thought of murmuring or remonstrating. He did not return until morning, and then he brought some one with him, wrapped in shawls and blankets—his patient—whom he lifted carefully from the carriage in his strong arms, carried gently into the house and laid on a bed, in a room which had long been unoccupied, but which Mrs. Annesley, at her husband's request, had prepared for an invalid inmate, that very morning.

About half an hour after this arrival, Dr. Annesley entered his father's chamber. He found the good old man sitting by his window, reading over the Psalms, in a low, fervent tone. He was so absorbed that he did not notice the approach of his son, till a hand was laid gently on his shoulder.

"Why bless me, Hugh," he exclaimed, "how you startled me! pray what brings you here so early?"

"Unusual business, dear father," replied the Doctor, "I have something of much moment to tell you. Do you think you can bear it?"

"I will try," answered the old man bracing himself, yet trembling visibly.

"Well, father, the young sailor whom I was called to see last night, was—"

"Oh, I know! I know! my poor, lost boy! my Philip!" cried Sir Hugh, covering his pale face with his hands. "Is he dead?"

"No, dear father, and he may possibly recover. He is very penitent and sorrowful. He says he would have written to you long ago, if he had dared—that he was on the way home when he was taken ill—coming to entreat your forgiveness, and that if you will grant it to him now, he can die content."

"And he shall have it!" cried Sir Hugh, "for I too often erred through over-indulgence, and sometimes through over-severity. I will go to him at once. Get me my cloak, my hat!"

"You will not need them," said the Doctor, smiling; "Philip is in his old room."

When the father and brother reached the bedside of the young sailor, they found that he had fallen asleep. He looked very ill; his sun-burnt face had grown almost fair in his long sickness—his sunken cheeks were slightly flushed with fever, and his long hair was scattered in disorder over the pillow.

As Sir Hugh gazed upon the sad face before him, he seemed to see in it the face of his dear dead wife, and what was more strange, that of his first-born son who died in early childhood.

When at length the young man opened his eyes, and saw his father bending over him, he seemed frightened and turned away his face. But the old man clasped him tenderly in his arms, as though he had been a child, and murmured with tears, "Philip, my son, my darling boy! I thank God, who has given you back to me!"

"Oh, father! do you indeed forgive me for all, *all?*" cried poor Philip, winding his thin arms about his old father's neck.

"As I hope to be forgiven," said Sir Hugh, solemnly.

They kept not exactly a "merry," but a very happy Christmas that season at Annesley House. There were no invited guests present, but Uncle Philip, now convalescent, left his chamber for the first time that evening, and was wheeled in his easy chair into the noble old dining-hall, to the boundless delight of the children.

"Mamma," said Herbert softly, "how young and handsome Grandpapa looks to-night!"

"I know why," said little Harry, with a very wise look, "it's all for Uncle Philip; 'cause he's getting well, and 'cause he wasn't drowned in the great deep sea!"

When Dr. Annesley came to read a portion of Scripture for the evening service, Philip, who sat close beside his aged father, said, shading his face with his hand, "Brother, will you please to read the parable of the Prodigal Son."

When the Doctor ceased reading, he saw that Philip had dropped his face on his father's shoulder, and that the old man had laid his hand on his son's head, and was looking upward for God's blessing on the repentant prodigal. And God did bless him, and made him ever after a faithful son and a good man. And God blessed all that household, for they loved him and one another, and strove to do good to all the world.

Snowdrop.

Little Nannie Tompkins was the daughter of a poor laborer, who lived in a humble cottage, by the roadside, near a small market-town, in the north of England. Nannie had two brothers older than herself, away at service, and a sister about two years younger, a gentle, pretty child, whose name was Olive —but she was always called Ollie.

The Tompkinses were the tenants of Farmer Grey, a good, amiable man, kind to the poor, and very tender to little children, birds, and animals—to everything that needed help and protection.

One chilly day, in the early spring, as Nannie was out in the fields, searching along the brooks for cresses, and under the hedges for the first violets, she met Farmer Grey, carrying a little lamb in his arms. He said he had found it in the field, curled down against its dead mother, and perishing with hunger and cold.

Seeing Nannie looking wistfully at the lamb, he said—

"If I will give you this poor little creature, will you feed it, and keep it warm, and try to raise it?"

"Oh, yes, indeed I will—thank you kindly, sir," she joyfully replied; and he put the lamb in her arms, and she wrapt it carefully in her cloak, and ran home with it.

Nannie's mother warmed some milk for the new pet, and fed him. Then she made him a nice soft bed near the fire, and before night he stopped shivering, and grew so strong that he was able to stand on his slender little legs, though rather unsteadily at first; and, the next day, he was running and playing about the house.

The children called this lamb, *Snowdrop*, both because he was so snowy white and delicate, and because he had been found in the early spring.

Well, Snowdrop grew and flourished, and proved himself to be a remarkably clever and lovable pet. He was very fond of the children, especially of Nannie, who was more tender and motherly toward him than her thoughtless little sister. And, next to her parents, and brothers, and Ollie, Nannie certainly loved her lamb. She fed him, washed him, played with him, and took him with her wherever she went. At night, he slept on his little bed of straw and old clothes in her chamber; and, in the morning, when he awoke, he would go tap-tapping over the floor to her bedside, put up his nose against her cheek, and cry, "Ma!" Nannie always wakened at this, and, after embracing her pet, got up and dressed directly.

One sunny May morning, as Nannie and Ollie sat before the cottage door, with their playmate, a neighbor's daughters—pretty Susan Smith and her little sister Mollie, came up, and stopped for a moment to speak to the children.

These girls were going to market; Susan, with a cage full of young pigeons on her head, and Mollie carrying a basket of fresh eggs.

Susan was a merry, teasing girl, and she began to advise Nannie to take the lamb to market, and sell him.

"Seeing that he is so fat and clean, he will be sure to fetch a good price," she said.

Nannie was shocked at this, and throwing her arms about her pet, she cried—

"I wouldn't sell my darling Snowdrop to a naughty, cruel butcher, for all the world! I'll never, *never* let him be killed!"

While the girls were talking, young Robert Grey, the farmer's son, rode up on his pretty black horse, and stopped too; it may be because of Susan Smith— for the two were famous friends. He heard Nannie's reply about the lamb, and looking down kindly upon her, said—

"If you are ever obliged to part with your pretty pet, my little girl, you need not sell him to the butcher, but bring him up to the farm-house, and I will buy him, and he shall not be killed."

Nannie thanked him very prettily, and he rode away with the merry market girls.

A few days after this, little Ollie was taken down with a fever, and was very ill for several weeks. At last, she began to get well very slowly; and then came the hardest time for her mother and sister—for she was fretful, dainty, and babyish, and cried a great deal for luxuries which her poor parents were not able to purchase for her. One afternoon, she cried incessantly for some strawberries, for she had heard they were in market. Strawberries are very dear in England, and Mrs. Tompkins could not buy them, for she had spent all her little stock of money for medicines; and now she felt so sad for the child that she could not help crying herself. When Nannie saw this, she put on her bonnet, and, calling Snowdrop, slipped away over the fields to the farm-house. When she came back, she was alone, but she put several bright shillings into her mother's hand, and choking down her sobs, said—

"There, mamma, I've done it! I've gone and sold Snowdrop—now take the money and buy Ollie the strawberries and other things."

Mrs. Tompkins kissed and blessed her "good little daughter," and went away and bought the fruit; and Ollie ate it eagerly and went to sleep very happy.

You may be very sure that Nannie did not eat any of the berries. She felt as though the smallest one among them would choke her. She did not utter a word of complaint, however, and kept back her tears till she went up to bed, alone. Then she could scarcely say her prayers for weeping, and when she came to repeat her sweet little evening hymn, she said the first lines in this way—

"Jesus, tender Shepherd, hear me,
Bless *my* little lamb to-night!"

Here she quite broke down, and was only able to sob out—

"Oh, yes, dear Jesus, do bless poor Snowdrop, for he's away off among strangers! Please to make people good to him—for you used to love little lambs and children too."

Just at this moment, Nannie heard a plaintive familiar cry—"Ma! Ma!" She sprang up from her knees, and ran to the window—and there, right down before her, in the moonlight, stood Snowdrop! In a minute, she had him in her arms, and was hugging him to her heart!

On the lamb's neck hung a little letter, saying that he was sent back as a present to Nannie, from Robert Grey.

I need hardly tell you that Snowdrop was never sold again. He lived with Nannie till she was a woman, and he a very venerable sheep; and then he died a peaceful death, and was buried in the garden, and real snowdrops grew over his grave.

My First day in Trowsers.

"Love was once a little boy," the old song says, and so was I; though I cannot flatter myself that beyond this there is any point of resemblance between Love and me,—stay, there is one strong one—I was extravagantly fond of shooting with a bow and arrow, and we all know that Love does nothing else but travel about shooting his little arrows into folks' hearts. *I* never shot anything but bull-frogs.

But I haven't got to my "trowsers" yet, have I? I don't see what made me think about Love here, for if poets and painters tell the truth, *he* never knew anything about trowsers—at least, he never *had* any.

I had toddled patiently through nearly four years of that period in the life of boys when there is little in their dress to distinguish them from girls, and which period is therefore a most aggravating memory to boys in general, when my mother astounded and delighted me one morning by the announcement that I was to have a pair of trowsers—that they were even then almost finished. What a whirl my little head was in all that day, to be sure! How my incipient manhood swelled and swaggered, impatient of the trammels of frocks and pantalettes! What dreams I had that night!

The next morning the trowsers came home, and had they been the jewelled robes in which I was to be proclaimed emperor of half the world, I could scarcely have looked upon them with more pleasure and pride— simple little India-nankeen trowsers, as they were, with buttons of pearl, and white embroidery of linen braid.

It was a bright morning in early June, and my mother decided that I might have them on at once. Oh, the pride of that day! What a space of time seemed to stretch between it and the yesterday! From what an airy height of scorn did I look down upon the whole race of frocks—even that one of crimson and black which only twenty-four short hours before, it had been the topmost delight of my little heart to be allowed to wear!

I was passed from hand to hand throughout the household—receiving admiring criticisms, and growing prouder and prouder; particularly when old Wangie, the cook, who was chief among my friends, exclaimed—"Bress de chile, he look grand as a king!"

I then begged my mother to let me sit out on the front step, "to see the wagons and folks go by," I said; but in reality, I am afraid, I only wanted to show my new trowsers. She said I might, and tied my hat on for me. I had not been there many minutes, before along came half a dozen of the youngest of the village boys, among them my cousin Philip, two years older than I. So long as I was in frocks, they had only condescended to greet me now and then in passing, with a—"Well, little 'un!"

But now I had emerged from the chrysalis of frocks—I was a boy—one of themselves, and entitled to consideration. So they stopped to talk with me, and look at my trowsers. They quite took down my pride by saying, in a patronizing tone—"They'll *do* for the first ones." But I remembered what Wangie had said, and managed to still keep up my grand feeling.

Presently they said they were going over into the meadow, to gather violets and buttercups, and asked me to go with them.

I said, quickly—"I'll go ask"—I was going to say "I'll go ask mother," but, just then, came the proud remembrance of my trowsers, and I thought to myself—"I am too big and too old to be asking mother every time I want to do anything; I'll go *without* asking." So I took Philip's hand, and off we started.

We went up a little hill and clambered through a fence, and there lay the meadow before us—oh, so lovely!—its rich robe of green grass pinned with buttercups—buttercups that seemed to have made captive the sunbeams that brought them life, so golden-bright and beautiful they were; and violets, upon which in tribute to their modesty, the sky had bestowed its color with its dew. Everything was in the first glad impulse of a new life.

The hill ran around two sides of this meadow, and right at the junction of the two sides, about half way down the slope, there was a little spring of clearest, coolest water. The half of a small barrel, with the head knocked out, had been sunk down about the fountain, and the space around it filled in tightly with gravel. By this means the little spring was forced to fill up the barrel, into which the people dipped their pitchers and buckets, before it got a chance to go idling, and singing, and splashing, as it did afterwards, away through the green grass, over the white pebbles, to the great dark woods beyond the meadow.

The owner of this spring, to protect it from the sun in hot weather, and to keep the cows away from it, when they were pasturing in the meadow, had built a little stone wall and arch around and partly over the barrel. The front part of this wall slanted backward (like the top of a gig or chaise when it is pushed half way back), so that the top of the archway, which was nicely sodded and seemed like a part of the hill, came directly over the barrel; to this front wall an old outside cellar-door had been hung; but rust and much use had broken its hinges, and, at the time I write of, it had to be lifted off and on. That morning, for some reason, they had not put it on, after getting water, but had left it up on the archway, with about one-third of it reaching over the edge.

After we had tired of gathering flowers, we all went up to this spring to drink, and see an old bull-frog that had lived there all alone for years. He used to sit up in a dark corner, on a large stone, all the summer through. He had never, in the memory of the oldest of us, been seen anywhere but upon that one stone, and he sat so still that he seemed more like a statue of a frog, than a real, live one. After sunset, above all the other "voices of the night," you could hear his deep bass through half the length of the village. We used to call him the village "Watchman," because his croaking sounded so exactly like the cry of watchmen—"All's well!" "All's well!"

I had heard Philip describe the "Watchman's" great eyes that never winked, and his ghostly stillness; I had heard his cry too, and it was with not a little awe—I am not sure there was not some *fear* mixed with the awe—that I approached the domicil of this village-wonder—this patron-saint of the spring. Philip pointed up into the dark corner, and at first I could only see two great solemn eyes; but presently I could make out the white throat, webbed feet, and dingy green back of the famous animal.

I was rather disappointed that he was not bigger and fiercer looking, for I had fancied that he must be something like the great dragon with which St. George had such a terrible time, only more tame, and not *quite* so big. But there was something in his quiet, steady look that I could not get my eyes away from; so I looked at him and he looked at me, till Philip took me by the hand, saying—"Come; we're going to sit up on the old door there, in the sun, and try who likes butter."

We all got seated on the door, and they proceeded to test each other's love for butter, by holding a buttercup under their chins. If it made a golden reflection upon their throats, it was a sure sign they *did* like butter; if it made no reflection, then they did *not* like it.

After it was decided that I had a strong regard for butter, my thoughts returned to the old bull-frog, and I crawled along to that corner of the door which overhung the spring, and lay down flat on my stomach, to get a good view of him. I had not lain there long before the boys got through with their buttercup experiment, and proposed to go home, as it was nearly dinner-time, they thought. With one accord they jumped off the door, and, quick as a flash, it tilted up, and headforemost I went, for all the world just like a bull-frog, plump into the spring!

The barrel was not wide enough for me to turn around in, even if I had thought of it. But I only thought, for an instant, how bright and pretty the sandy bottom was, through which the up-springing water came bubbling softly against my lips and cheek—then my head seemed to become very full —I felt as though I were choking, and there was a sound in my ears like that of a wind in the woods; then everything grew dark and seemed to stop. The boys were so frightened they could do nothing, and there I stuck. There I might have stuck till my little legs had grown so stiff, and still, and cold, that it had been beyond the power of even India-nankeen trowsers to wake them into life, and warmth, and vanity again.

But, happily for me, there was a woman spinning just outside the door of the little house on the hill, who, with the instinctive watchfulness which mothers have for all children, had kept her eye upon us all the time, and when I was tilted into the spring, she ran quickly down, seized me by the heels, drew me out, and carried me, all white and cold as death, to my mother. By the time she reached our house, there was a little fluttering of the heart, which, after they had rubbed me awhile with flannels dipped in hot rum, gradually increased to the usual regular beat; soon the lips grew red again, and directly the eyes opened. They were a little vacant and glassy at first, and I felt bewildered, but it was not long before I remembered all about the whole affair.

The first words I spoke were to ask about my trowsers. They brought them in to me, all wet and soiled, where they had rubbed against the green sedges about the spring. The sight of them in this condition distressed me so much that old Wangie, who had been running about wringing her hands and crying —"Oh, little massa am dead, sartin!"— but who was now overjoyed to find that I was not, declared they should be washed and ironed that very day. She started off with them in such a hurry that she trod on the tail of her favorite cat, Jim, who was washing his face with his paw by the door. Wangie (bless her old black face!—she's dead now;) would have stopped and petted the poor cat, usually, but this time to the great astonishment of all, for she had the kindest heart in the world, she gave him a prodigious kick, which sent him full two yards down the hall.

My mother had learned all about the accident from the boys and the woman who saved me, and when, after a few hours, I was able to get up, she took me quietly into her room and explained to me how wrong it was to go over to the meadow without asking her permission, and told me that, although I had been pretty severely punished already, yet, in order to make me remember never to do so again, she should put my trowsers away in the drawer for two weeks, during which I was to wear frocks again.

What a blow was this to me! How all my pride and glory of the morning were humbled to the earth! All the little world of hopes and vanities which my foolish heart had wrought, was scattered to chaos again! I bore up under it pretty well the rest of the day, ate my supper in silence, and went quietly to bed; but after mother had gone down, and I was left alone, I could stand it no longer. I lay there in the dark sobbing and sobbing, till I sobbed myself to sleep.

So ended *my first day in trowsers*!

The Stolen Birds' Nest.

"In these summer bushes
Listen to the thrushes—
Hear the robin and the wren call from tree to tree:
Hear how all day long
The woods o'erflow with song,
And how every leafy branch blooms with melody!
Do you not feel sorry,
Seeing me in sadness,
When the other little birds are so full of gladness?"

CLARENCE COOK.

In one of the sunniest and sweetest countries in the world, the south of France, lived my heroes, two little peasant boys, named Auguste and Leon Duval. Their fathers were brothers, and vine growers on the estate of the Count de Vallence. The little cousins were excellent friends, and almost always seen together, following their fathers through the beautiful vineyards, gathering up the branches which they had pruned away, or helping to pick grapes at vintage-time, or straying through the grand old woods of the chateau, searching after nuts and wild berries. They usually agreed very well, both in work and play, but they sometimes had their little quarrels like too many other children. Auguste was full two months the elder, and he was apt to presume upon that, and be proud and overbearing towards Leon. He was shrewd and somewhat selfish, and frequently took advantage of his cousin, who was almost too confiding and generous. They were beautiful boys; perhaps Auguste was the most admired of the two, for he had a rich brown complexion, with glowing cheeks and lips, glossy raven curls, and bold, black, handsome eyes. Leon was the fairer; he had brown hair, and deep, soft, brown eyes, which however, could flash in anger; lips like wild rose leaves, fresh and sweet, but which could curl in scorn at cruelty and meanness. Usually his face wore a very mild and amiable expression, and if Auguste was the most admired, Leon was the most loved.

In the woods of the chateau the cousins sometimes met the Countess Marie, the pretty young wife of the Count de Vallence, who loved to walk in the cool, green forest paths. She was attracted by the beauty, simplicity, and arch playful ways of the merry boys, and often whiled away an hour in talking with them and watching them in their sports. Once she took them with her to the chateau, and showed them the lofty rooms, the pictures, statues, fountains, and conservatories, enjoying much their wonder and pleasure. That which gave them most delight was the aviary, where there was a fine collection of talking and singing birds—magpies, parrots, macaws, canaries, goldfinches, English black-birds, and many other kinds. As they were looking at these, the countess said to the old servant who had charge of them,—"Pierre, why have we no robins?"

"I did not know that my lady would care for such common birds," answered the old man.

"Care for them! I think they are the sweetest songsters in the world. I once saw one at Paris that could sing several opera airs. Could you teach them to sing so, Pierre?"

"Yes, my lady, if I had them young," he replied.

"Well, then, we must have some," said the lady, decisively; "my bird-choir is not complete without them; so remember, Pierre!"

Just as the Countess was dismissing her little friends at the hall door, the Count de Vallence entered. He was a stern, haughty man, and now seemed astonished and shocked at seeing his countess making so much of a couple of peasant boys. He drew down his black eyebrows, and looked so grim, that they were glad to escape, and the good Countess never took them there again.

Shortly after this visit, it happened that one day while little Leon was alone in the woods, searching for berries, he discovered a nest of young robins, built in a snug, shady place, against a large branch of an old oak tree. Leon stood for a long time silently watching the little, downy, chirping things, and the happy parent-birds, who were bringing them food, and dropping it into their wide gaping bills. They patiently flew back and forth, and brought worms, flies, and berries, till the greedy little bills gaped and chirped no more—then the good father-bird perched on a limb above the nest, began singing a sweet, tender song, while the kind mother-bird brooded over her darlings, as the dewy twilight was coming on.

Leon was so delighted with his new-found treasure, that the next morning he brought his cousin to the spot. When Auguste saw the nest, his eye flashed with eager joy.

"Ah," he exclaimed, "how lucky we are to find a nest of young robins for the dear Countess! Let us take them to her, and she will give us more money than we have ever seen in the world;" and Auguste began immediately to climb the old oak tree.

"Oh don't, don't, cousin Auguste!" cried Leon, clinging about him. "It would be a cruel, wicked thing to steal away those poor little birds—don't you see how dearly the old birds love them?"

Auguste thrust him back, exclaiming angrily—"Didn't the Countess say she wanted some young robins for her aviary?—then how dare you say it would be wicked to get them for her!" But Leon answered sturdily—

"The good *curé* says God takes care of the birds—He gave the little robins to the old ones, just as He gave us to our fathers and mothers; so it *must* be wicked to steal them away. And now, cousin dear, do come down and let them be."

But Auguste had already grasped the nest. He tore it away from its place, and slid with it down the tree. The old birds flew about him in the utmost distress, uttering wild, piercing cries of fear and sorrow. Leon's tender heart was touched by their grief—he expostulated and pleaded with his cousin, and then, seeing that entreaties were in vain, grew very angry—he even doubled up his little fists, and was about to fight for the liberation of the tiny captives. But he remembered in time the pious teachings of his mother and the good *curé*, and returned home, with a swelling heart and tearful eyes, while his cousin hurried off to the chateau, with the robins.

When Leon told his mother the story of the birds, she was very indignant, and started to seek Auguste's father, and ask him to send after the cruel boy, and compel him to restore the young robins to the old ones, for her kind mother-heart felt for them very much. But when Leon told her that they were taken for the Countess, she sat down to her work again, and said it was all well, for she had a great awe of the great lady.

Leon hoped in his heart that the good Countess would refuse the birds, and send Auguste back with the nest; so he waited as patiently as he could for his cousin's return. He came back, however, without the nest, triumphantly jingling a handful of silver coin.

"See," he cried, "what the Countess gave me for the robins! Here, Leon, is your share."

Leon took the money, but only to fling it all indignantly at his cousin's feet, bursting into tears as he did so. Some may think I ought to be sorry to tell of this fit of passion in my noble little hero, but I am not. While the angry tears were yet flowing, he rushed out of his father's cottage, and ran towards the chateau. He did not stop to rest, or slacken his pace till he reached the great hall door. Then he paused, and the thought of the dusky arches of the old hall, hung with faded banners, and the grim statues in armor standing along its walls, and that stern, black-bearded Count, whom he might meet, almost took away his courage. He stood poised on the tips of his toes, with his hand on the great knocker, hesitating and fearing, when, all at once, he seemed to hear again the wild, mournful cry of the poor mother-robin!—then his heart grew brave, and he boldly sounded the knocker.

When a servant went to the Countess and told her that another little peasant boy wanted to see her, she happened to be in the nursery, paying a visit to her baby-son, the heir to the title and estates of the Count de Vallence. She was sitting by his side, fondly watching him, as he lay asleep in a beautiful little cradle, all satin and down, and fine linen and rich lace. The lady looked surprised when she saw Leon's flushed and tearful face.

"Why, my child," she said kindly, "what do you want of me?"

"I want those little birds," he replied rather bluntly.

"Those birds!" she answered, "why, did not Auguste give you part of the money? I told him to."

"I don't want any money," said Leon, "I want the birds back again. It wasn't good of you to buy them—their father and mother are grieving for them. It was a wicked thing to steal away their little ones, and the nice nest they had worked so hard to make. Aint you afraid that they will fly up to God and tell him all about it? And how would you feel to have some great giant's boy come and steal *your* little one, and carry it away in that pretty nest, there?"

At first, the Countess smiled at this earnest little speech—then the tears rushed to her eyes; she bent down and kissed her sleeping babe, then, turning to Leon, she laid her hand caressingly on his head, saying, "I thank you, my dear child, for the lesson you have taught me. Surely you shall have the little robins back again. I have done wrong to buy them. I ask pardon of you, and of God."

"And of the birds," added Leon.

"And of the birds," repeated the Countess, smiling a little at the child's simplicity.

So Leon received the nest of little young robins, and took it safely back to the old oak tree in the forest. He stopped on the way to dig some worms, with which he fed his little feathered friends, who were getting quite clamorous with hunger. When he had fixed the nest securely in its old place, he hid himself in a clump of bushes near by, to watch for the coming of the old birds. All the afternoon he watched and waited, and still they did not come.

At last, when it was almost twilight—the time for flowers and little birds to go to sleep, he saw the two robins—he was sure they were the same birds—come slowly winging their way towards the oak. It seemed they could not sleep away from their home, although it had been made so desolate. The male bird flew in among the upper branches, and perched on one of them; but the female bird stopped in a tree near by. It appeared that she was hardly equal to the sight of the dear old place.

Soon Leon saw the male bird flutter on his perch, and turn his head quickly this way and that. He had heard those little complaining voices chirping below him!—then he darted downward and hovered over the nest a moment, to be sure they were all there, then flew to his mate, to tell her the glad news. In another moment, they were both back by the nest, hopping and hovering about it—chirping joyfully and lovingly in answer to the eager little chirps of their young ones. Late as it was, they flew about, and got up a nice little supper of worms for their darlings. After that, while the mother-bird spread over them her soft warm wings, and hushed them to sleep with the happy beating of her heart, the father bird flew up to a branch above them, and burst into a glad, delicious song.

"He is thanking God," said Leon softly to himself, reverently taking off his little cap, and making the sign of the cross—"he is thanking God."

The Story of Grace Darling.

On the lonely little island of Brownsman, one of the Farne group, on the coast of Northumberland, England, lived William Darling, lighthouse keeper, a brave, honest, intelligent man. Grace, his daughter, the youngest of seven children, was courageous like her father, good and gentle like her mother. She was a quiet, modest girl, with a slender form, a beautiful face, and the sweetest smile in the world.

The Farne Islands are very wild and desolate, being little better than piles of black rocks towering above the dismal, roaring seas of that stormy and perilous coast. In calm weather they are surrounded by a fringe of white surf, and in times of storm they are almost overwhelmed by the great, raging surges. Through the channels between these islands the sea rushes like swollen torrents; and here, before beacons were built upon the rocks, occurred many shipwrecks. Even now they are very dangerous spots, for in spite of those friendly lights glimmering through the blackness of the tempest and the night, the force of the gale will sometimes drive vessels headlong upon the rocks, dash them to pieces, and scatter them over the boiling deep.

The Brownsman was the outermost of the Farne Islands—the last rocky foothold of human life; and beyond it was a vast expanse—and an awful depth of sea. It had scarcely any vegetation, but stood out from the water, bare and black and bleak. The jagged cliffs, and dim, sounding caves, were alive with seabirds—almost the only living creatures to be seen on the island, out of the family at the lighthouse.

In this strange, lonely place, Grace Darling passed her earliest years. She was a shy and thoughtful child, and learned to take pleasure in the wild and dreary scenery around her. Shut out from the world, as she and her dear ones were, it seemed to her they were all the nearer heaven;—denied social pleasures and consolations even while living, toiling, watching for their fellow beings, she felt that God would remember them and protect them. To her the black stone hills of those desolate islands, standing bare-headed under the gray sky, were grander than towers or cathedrals could be; and the stars and the moon shone as tenderly above the wild, rough perch on the lighthouse rock, as on palaces and sweet Italian gardens.

She loved the lighthouse, the guide and saviour of tempest-tossed mariners. She loved the labors of her brave father, and the sports of her hardy brothers; she loved the shy sea-birds—some of these she tamed, by gentle advances and companionship, till they would stoop their swift wild wings to her hand. She loved the sea when it was calm—when the bright waves came running up the sandy beach, and seemed to prostrate themselves before her, caressing her small white feet with soft, cool kisses; and in storm she did not fear it. When it would break on the rocks with a hoarse, threatening sound, and dash over her a shower of angry spray, she would laugh and say, "Roar away, old sea! I am sure you wouldn't be in such a rage if the winds hadn't provoked you. By and by you will get good, and feel sorry, and creep up the sands all calm and smiling, to make friends with me again;—and I'll forgive you, you dear old sea, if you won't do any mischief now, and will leave me all the pretty shells and mosses you are tossing up on the shore."

And Grace dearly loved mosses and shells. She knew all the little caves and coves and sandy nooks where they were to be found, and the best time to look for them, and used to come home from her solitary rambles with her little apron full of treasures, dearer to her simple heart than rare exotics, or costly gems. She said the bright-colored mosses were sea-flowers, torn by the thieving waves out of the mermaids' gardens—and that the shells were the houses or pleasure-boats of the little sea-fairies.

So it was that Grace Darling was not discontented with her lot, nor with her lonely home, where love and God dwelt—did not fear tempest, nor night, nor raging seas, nor the world; but grew up courageous, trustful, unselfish, and "pure in heart."

When Grace was about eleven years old, her father removed from the lighthouse of the Brownsman to that of the Longstone, a neighboring island. And here it was, that on the 7th of September, 1838, when she was about twenty-two, she performed the heroic act which made her sweet name a blessed "household word" the world over.

The steamer *Forfarshire*, on her voyage from Hull to Dundee, in a terrible gale, struck on a rock amidst the Farne Islands. Immediately a portion of the crew, cowardly and selfish men, lowered the long-boat, leapt into it, and left the captain, his wife, their comrades, and all the passengers, to their fate! In a short time, a huge wave lifted up the entire vessel, then, letting it fall violently, broke it in two parts upon the sharp rock. The after part, on which were the captain, his wife, and many passengers, was carried off and soon dashed to pieces—the fore part, on which were five of the crew and four passengers, remained on the rock. In the little fore cabin, into which every now and then washed the waves, was a woman by the name of Sarah Dawson, with two young children—and piteously, hour after hour, came up to those on deck, the frightened cries of the poor creatures down there in the dark and cold alone. But by and by those cries died away and were still.

The sufferers remained on the wreck, exposed to the fury of the tempest, and expecting every minute to be washed away, all that long, long night. In the morning they were seen from the Longstone lighthouse, about a mile distant. Only Mr. Darling, his wife, and daughter Grace were at home. The storm had somewhat abated, yet the sea ran high, and the surf around the islands and hidden rocks seemed dashing up into the very clouds. It was dark and misty, and the sufferers on the wreck could be but dimly seen through the distance and the storm. Yet Grace saw them clear enough with her tender, sympathizing *heart*—saw all their peril, their fear, their agony, and, looking into her father's face, she said firmly—

"Papa, those poor people *must* be saved!"

Mr. Darling shook his head sadly, and then she added,

"You and I must do it. We will go to them in our boat—we can perhaps bring them all away in that."

"Impossible, my child—no boat could live in such a sea. We must leave them in God's hands!"

"No, papa, God has given them into ours; and He will protect us in seeking to rescue them—we can but try."

So Grace won over her father to her noble undertaking, and they two launched the boat, and rowed off bravely toward the wreck. Mrs. Darling not only did not object to their going, though she knew all the dreadful peril of their enterprise, but helped to launch the boat. I think she was not less heroic than either her husband or her daughter.

It was ebb tide, or the boat could not have passed between the islands—but it would be flowing before they could hope to return, which would render it impossible for them to row up to their island alone—so unless they could reach the wreck, and get rowers from there, they would be obliged to stay outside till the next ebb tide, exposed to the greatest peril. All this they knew.

The most serious danger they incurred was that of their boat being dashed by the furious waves so violently against the rock on which the ship had struck, as to break it to pieces instantly. As they drew near, Grace's firm lips moved in prayer, and her father's weather-browned face grew pale. But the same good God who had guided them through the wild white surf, and over the treacherous hidden reefs, sent a smooth strong wave, that gently lifted the prow of their boat on to the rock.

They reached the wreck in safety, to the unspeakable joy and amazement of the poor people there. In the cabin they found Mrs. Dawson, nearly dead, with her arms clasped about her two children, both quite dead. All were lowered into the boat, and safely rowed to the Longstone, where Mrs. Darling received them warmly, and cared for them with motherly tenderness.

Grace, when she reached the lighthouse, was much exhausted with rowing, and almost fell into her mother's arms as she stepped ashore. But she roused her energies, and nerved her noble heart anew, for the sake of the poor sufferers. Without waiting to remove her own wet clothes, or even to wring the sea-water from her long dark hair, she devoted herself to their relief and comfort. She gathered them around the fire—she gave them food, warm drink and dry clothing. Very tenderly she consoled those who had lost property and friends by the wreck. She took the hands of old seamen who had grown as weak as women through suffering, and told them of One who pitied them, "even as a father pitieth his children." She took the childless Mrs. Dawson in her arms, laid her poor distracted head on her breast, and wept with her.

The storm continued so violent that the sufferers were obliged to remain at the lighthouse for several days, as were also a boat's crew who came to their rescue from North Sunderland, too late, and could not return. Yet all were treated most hospitably and kindly—Grace gave up her bed to poor Mrs. Dawson, and slept on a table.

At last the storm passed over, and was succeeded by calm and sunshine—the ship-wrecked guests went to their homes, some rejoicing and some sorrowing, but all bearing hearts warm with gratitude toward their deliverers. Doubtless some of those rescued men and women are yet living, and perhaps on stormy nights, when the winds roar and the sea thunders against the rocky shore, they gather their children or grandchildren about them and tell the story of the wreck of the *Forfarshire*, of their awful peril and wonderful deliverance.

Grace Darling and her father would soon have forgotten their heroic act had they been left to do so. But the people they had saved, in their gratitude and wonder, told the story wherever they went. Accounts of it appeared in all the papers, and flew over the world. The bleak island and lonely lighthouse were visited by thousands, eager to get a sight of the noble heroine and her brave old father. Costly presents and tributes of admiration poured in upon them from all quarters. The Duke and Duchess of Northumberland invited them over to Alnwick Castle, and presented Grace with a gold watch;—the Humane Society passed a vote of thanks for her heroism, and sent her a handsome piece of plate. A public subscription was raised for her benefit, and amounted to about seven hundred pounds—some three thousand five hundred dollars.

All this fame and applause for what seemed to her a simple act of humanity, surprised and almost overwhelmed the modest girl. She shrank from the curious looks of strangers who thronged to see her, and became more shy and reserved than ever—she refused all invitations to go out into the world—but dividing many of her gifts between her brothers and sisters, she remained with her father and mother at the lighthouse, cheerfully fulfilling her humble domestic duties. God had made her very noble, and the whole world could not spoil her.

But not long was her beautiful, heroic life to brighten that lone and desolate spot. In the fall of 1841 she fell into delicate health, and symptoms of consumption soon manifested themselves. She was removed to the house of her sister at Bamborough, on the coast. It was thought she would get better when the Spring came—but it was not so. She still continued to fail—to fade and fade away. She was taken to Alnwick, from which she was to proceed to Newcastle for medical advice. While at Alnwick, the Duchess of Northumberland treated her with all a sister's kindness—sent her own physician to her—supplied her with every luxury, and better than all, went often to see her, very plainly dressed, and without a single attendant. She had the good sense to lay aside as it were, her coronet—forget her title before the better nobility of that dying girl—and so proved herself something far greater than a Duchess—a true and loving woman.

Grace was soon taken back to Bamborough, that she might meet death with all her loved ones around her. And there, in the place where she was born, she died, on the 20th of October, 1842. She took leave of all her friends calmly, and very tenderly—giving to each one something to keep in remembrance of her—then meekly folded her hands on her breast, and slept in God's peace. She was buried within sound of the sea—within sight perhaps of the lighthouse, and the rock of the wreck—and the sea seems to mourn for her now, and the lighthouse and the rock are her monuments.

Yet, though Grace Darling should be forgotten on earth, though the lighthouse should fall—the rock crumble away—the sea cease to murmur of her—her name shall not perish, for it is written in the Lord's "Book of Life," and she dwells now where storms and death cannot come, and where "there is no more sea."

Hymn,

WRITTEN FOR A SABBATH SCHOOL PIC-NIC.

Our dear Lord Jesus, thou didst call
  Young children once to thee—
Didst hold them in thy loving arms,
  And bless them tenderly;—
Now, like those children, let us come
  And gather round thy knee.

Oh teach us that God dwelleth here—
  These woods his leafy shrines—
That incense rises from the flowers,
  And fragrant swinging vines,
And wordless psalms swell up from out
  The solemn sounding pines.

Oh teach us to behold where'er
  Our joyous footsteps rove,
The emblems of a Father's care
  And tokens of his love—
In sunshine smiling on the sward,
  In clouds that brood above.

His glory in the golden morn,
  His peace in noon's repose,
His goodness in the twilight shades
  That softly round us close—
"The beauty of his holiness"
  In every wilding rose.

Oh hear our hymn and bless our feast,
  And smile upon our play—
Oh fill our hearts with thy dear love,
  And keep us glad and gay,
And sinless as the little birds,
  Throughout this summer day.

THE END.

Lightning Source UK Ltd.
Milton Keynes UK
UKHW041046100820
367987UK00004B/1157